I0682483

# The Promise
# in a
# Brown Paper Bag

**Bob Richey**

Copyright © 2025 by Bob Richey

All rights reserved.

No part of this publication may be reproduced,
distributed, or transmitted in any form or by any
means, including photocopying, recording, or other
electronic or mechanical methods, without the prior
written permission of the publisher, except as
permitted by U.S. copyright law. For permission
requests, contact Bob@Bob-Richey.com

The story, all names, characters, and incidents
portrayed in this production are fictitious. No
identification with actual persons (living or
deceased), places, buildings, and products are
intended or should be inferred.

TWISTED TRUTH
PRESS

Published by:

Book Cover by 'Zsa Zsa'

ISBN   978-1-970990-03-4 Paperback

Second Edition 2025

# DEDICATION

This book is dedicated to anyone who has had any paranormal experience; to anyone who has felt a supernatural presence; to the people who believe in angels. Whether you have felt a strange cold draft or heard a voice when you were alone, only you will understand the makings of this book. I don't believe in any of these superstitions. I am more a man of science. I have, however, had a few supernatural events, and I have seen both UFOs and ghosts. I've personally experienced unusual and unbelievable happenings. I don't believe in any of them, except I continue to knock on wood, and I refuse to take down my dreamcatcher because I have only had good dreams since I put it up years ago.

This book is from one of those dreams.

# The Promise in a Brown Paper Bag

## Preface

As stated in the dedication, this book came to me in a series of dreams. It wasn't a real dream, a sound asleep, waking and trying to remember and piece the abstract images back together kind of dream. Rather, it was an unusually clear, linear story playing out in my mind as I was awakening in the morning. I rolled over thinking that it was odd, and fell back asleep. When I woke, another part had played out. Then a third, and then the finish.

The finish tied the dream all together. I immediately thought that it was a gift. Someone had given me their story. I turned on the computer and wrote it down. It took me two hours to type it out as I tried to remember the story exactly as it was told to me. I didn't edit it other than spelling, and I made some changes only because I realized I didn't know the a children's book, but I was moved to tears at times while transcribing it. To repeat, I wrote this linear from start to gender. I was never told if it was a little girl or a little boy. The story came through like end just like I dreamed it. I did not go back and fix it up or edit it. A copy of that writing is included in the back of the book. You should read it after enjoying this story I have created, The Promise in a Brown Paper Bag, which uses the dream as a guideline.

I can see the pictures of this story clearly, even now. The images in my mind of the story get more vivid and beautiful as the story progresses. I didn't realize that until the next day.

Nothing in the story has to do with me. I have never thought about the subject or had any ideas to write a story remotely like this. I don't know why I dreamed this dream.

# The Promise in a Brown Paper Bag

# Chapter 1

## A Young Doctor

Thomas Betterman MD. General Surgeon, Floor-2, Room-6

The Assistant Secretary to the Head Administrator, Ms. Julia Wright, had just finished adding his name to the first floor directory next to the main elevators when the newest "Hope Children's Hospital" doctor entered the hospital lobby.

"Good morning, Julia," the young doctor said.

"Well, good morning, Doctor Thomas," she replied. "I've just finished adding your name."

"I see! Thank you very much. It looks perfect," the new doctor added.

Thomas pushed the button and proceeded up to his new office. He thought about Julia as he went up. She was an excellent secretary, and he would need someone like her to run his new office. He would also need an assistant to help with the new patients.

Thomas entered his new office and looked around. He pushed the desk from the middle of the room and positioned it to immediately face the entrance door. A landline phone was the only other item in the room besides some waiting room chairs. He went through the double doors and saw that the nurse assistant area was in the same condition. He peered into the restroom, and it was sparkling clean; it even had a little shelf with a door that connected to the nurse's area. Great, he thought.

He continued by inspecting the two examination rooms and was pleased. The hall ended at the back door to his office. He went in and immediately opened the other main door. It connected to the back of the nurse's station. This will do nicely, he thought, and he sat down at his new desk.

There was a directory booklet next to his phone, and he looked up, then called Julia Wright.

"Do you have any applicants you could recommend for my secretary?" Thomas asked.

"Yes, Doctor Thomas," she replied. "I have a list, but there is one in particular I have in mind if you wish to trust my intuition."

"Yes, indeed! Send her up as soon as possible."

"I'll call her now!" she ended.

The new doctor went into each room and wrote down the equipment and computers he would need. When he finished, he returned to his office and called maintenance to set up installations.

As he was finishing, he heard a noise from the other room. He got up and went through the nurse's station into the reception area. Listening, he heard a slight knock on the door. He opened the door.

"Hi, Julia sent me up to interview for the secretary position!" She looked right into his eyes and smiled.

Thomas smiled right back and said, "Come in, come in, have a seat, sit right there at this desk," as he pointed to the desk and phone.

He pulled a waiting room chair in front of the desk and sat down. When she was seated, he asked her the first question.

"If you get the job as secretary, what would be the first thing that you would do?"

"The first thing I would do, if you hire me, would be to put a big sign on the door that says 'Welcome! Come On In.'"

"Great answer!" he replied. "My second and last question is, what is your name?"

"Oh! I'm so sorry!" she said as she extended her hand to shake. "Nancy May Johnson. But everyone calls me May."

"Okay, May, after you order the sign for the door, I'll need you to call maintenance and get them to send up a decorator to spruce this place up. Make sure the janitors put us in their rotation and..."

May interrupted him right there.

"It will be my job and my privilege to anticipate and handle any and all of this office's needs. We'll be up and running at light speed. You have my word!" May explained.

"Thank you," Thomas answered. "One last thing. Call Julia and have her send up applicants for my nurse assistant. You will vet them, and if someone seems right, have them wait and I will see them right away."

"I'll actually do that first," she smiled.

"You're going to work out just fine," Thomas concluded.

The rest of the week was bustling as workers delivered, cleaned, and installed all the equipment and amenities that were needed for a surgeon's practice.

# The Promise in a Brown Paper Bag

On Monday morning, everything was in place and ready. May had even scheduled patients starting in the afternoon.

Thomas came out of his newly decorated office and confronted May.

"You have scheduled patients and we don't have a nurse yet!" he exclaimed.

"Doctor Thomas, I must explain something. I was going to let her explain, but it now seems I must tell you."

"Tell me what?" he asked.

"Doctor, I hired a nurse assistant for you on my first day. She had to give a week's notice on her last job. She will be here any minute, and I'm sure you will approve. She dropped everything for the opportunity to come work here with me for you. Her name is Christine."

But before she could finish, the door opened and May stepped in.

"May?" the doctor quizzed.

"No, I'm Christine, but call me Chris," she answered. "Yes, May and I are identical twins. I've come because you need my help and I need to help someone starting out. I want to start at the beginning, and working with my sister May is a dream come true."

"Well, I for one am not going to ruin a dream come true, so go get ready for our first patient this afternoon," Thomas instructed. He looked at May and gave her a big smile, and she returned it right back at him.

The place was abuzz with activity; the two girls worked together printing, filing, and getting the place ready. The girls worked together like clockwork, and everything was in place and ready when the first patient walked in the door.

# Chapter 2

## A Young Girl

Each morning, the doctor walked the quarter mile down the street to the bus stop. It wasn't much of a street, as it was more of a hardpan road. It didn't have a sidewalk or amenities like a curb or drainage, but it was labeled a street on the map, so everyone referred to it as such. Thomas lived on the end of this dead-end street in the largest house with the biggest yard. Even the trees were the biggest in the area. He had inherited it from his late parents, and, being an only child, lived alone in this big old house. He had walked down this street throughout university and continued all through interning at the Hope Children's Hospital. He was now walking down this street every workday as he started his private practice at the hospital.

Almost every day, while walking down the street, he would see a young girl sitting in the window waving at him. He always waved back at her. Sometimes, on the days she wasn't there, he would pause and shuffle his feet for a while, giving her time to come to the window and wave. It worked some of the time, and he would wave and continue with his day. He had never seen her in the window on the way home until that day. She was waving and smiling, and he was waving back when he decided to go to the door.

Thomas knocked briskly at the door, and it was quickly opened by a woman in a faded dress. She had a raw beauty covered up with a lifetime of hardship.

# The Promise in a Brown Paper Bag

She was holding a needle and thread and, while smiling politely, said, "Hello!"

"Hello, I'm Doctor Thomas Betterman, and I live at the end of the street," he said as he introduced himself.

"Oh, I know who you are, Thomas. K

now it or not, you are the talk of this little road, and I am pleased to meet you," she continued. "You are often the talk of this house too; it would be always if Suzie had her way."

"Is Suzie the girl in the window I always wave at?" he asked.

"Oh yes, she talks about you all the time. I'm her mother, Isabel."

"Can she come out here so I can meet her proper at last?" he asked.

"No! She must stay in bed. She is too sick to come out here, but you are welcome to come in and meet her in her room, if you wish."

"Of course I will," he replied. "Has she always been sick? Is that why I never see her outside playing? Take me to her, please."

"Come this way." Isabel motioned, and he followed her to Suzie's room.

Suzie's room was somewhat dark. The large maple trees in the front yard shaded most of the light from entering her room, even though there was a large window next to her bed. As he peered in, he immediately noticed the many drawings taped to the walls. It was obvious that Suzie spent a lot of time drawing, and the pictures were very detailed and beautifully proportioned. It was apparent that she loved to draw and that she had a lot of talent for her young age.

The Promise in a Brown Paper Bag

Once their eyes met, Suzie started crying and reached out both arms to hug him. He hurried ahead and bent down on one knee and gave her a hug, quietly saying, "Don't cry." She continued to cry and showed no sign of letting go of the hug. But soon, even this was too strenuous for her, and she slowly released Thomas and laid back onto the bed to catch her breath.

"She knew you would come," Isabel said, "she always knew you would come."

"She always says you will come to save her," echoed a small boy's voice. Melvin, her one-year-older brother, had peeked into the room, mostly hidden by his mom. "That's the only game she ever wants to play. She has the girl doll and I have the boy doll, and she always says, 'Did you come to save me?' And I have to say, 'Yes, I've come to save you.'" Young Melvin continued, "Every day the same game over and over. I'm sure glad you finally came! Maybe now we can play a different game? One I like for a change!"

The doctor smiled and focused on Suzie. "Is that what you think?"

Suzie smiled and, still crying, explained that that's what she has always dreamed. That for as long as she could remember, she dreamed that he would stop and come into her room to save her. Suzie said, "I knew you would come. I always knew you would come."

Doctor Thomas reached down and gave her another hug. "You knew this all the time? This is your dream? Who am I to say no? Starting tomorrow, I will start to find out what is wrong and learn what needs to be done. Okay? You rest now."

"I know, I know. I already know!" she replied.

Thomas talked to Isabel and explained that in the morning he would send a driver from the hospital with a wheelchair to come and get them. She would be his first patient of the day, and he would do everything he could to help her. He gave her his card and said she could call him anytime. Isabel waved goodbye and returned to her sewing. The new doctor started to walk the rest of the way home. He quickly stopped and walked backwards, counting his steps aloud, "one, two, three, four, five, six, seven." He looked over, and there she was, waving at him and both smiling and crying. He smiled and waved and continued home with a newfound spring in his step.

Suzie called Melvin and pleaded with him to bring her some paper and crayons, and after tormenting her a bit, he relented and brought her the supplies. She started drawing, knowing exactly what she wanted to draw. Soon a picture of a handsome young doctor kneeling beside the bed took shape. She was exhausted from the excitement of the day, but she pushed through the tiredness and completed the artwork. She carefully taped it to the wall next to her pillow, staring at it as she fell asleep.

# Chapter 3

## Examination

The next morning saw a large black car pull up and park outside their house. A tall young man dressed in all blue scrubs from the hospital got out and retrieved a wheelchair from the trunk. Isabel was waiting in the doorway. Motioning him to come in, he wheeled the chair to the doorway, only to realize that the doorways and hallway were too narrow for the chair. Suzie watched as he returned to the car and placed the wheelchair back into the trunk. Her heart sank as she realized that there was a problem. She carefully watched as he came back into the house and appeared in her bedroom doorway. "The wheelchair is too big," he explained. "Would it be alright if I carried you to the car instead?"

"Oh yes," she exclaimed, "Please carry me to the car!" Suzie was relieved that she was still going to see Doctor Thomas. She reached out both arms, and the orderly from the hospital scooped her up into his arms. He effortlessly carried her to the car while Isabel held open the door. Isabel slid into the back seat with Suzie and comforted her daughter.

The ride to the hospital was wonderful. It was a late spring morning and, although it was a bit chilly, the sun had already been sending its warming rays into the car. Isabel was accustomed to taking the bus at the bus stop at the end of the street just like Thomas, so the ride in a car was unusual. This ride in the car, in the backseat, with a driver seemed exquisite.

They watched out the window, pointing out things that they saw to each other, and completely forgot the gravity of this trip.

Soon they arrived at the main entrance. Both Julia and Christine were waiting. Chris was holding a wheelchair and the orderly got out and introduced her to Isabel. He then turned and picked up Suzie and transferred her to the chair. Suzie didn't mind as some might think. She looked at the orderly and liked his smile. He was strong and handsome too. He wasn't Doctor Thomas handsome, of course, but he would do for now.

They wheeled Suzie into the lobby, and Julia casually said, "Come see me after work, May, I have something to discuss with you." Christine just smiled and boarded the elevator.

Upon opening the door, Christine introduced Isabel and Suzie; they both marveled at the likenesses of the twin girls. Christine just smiled and spoke. "Oh, Julia wants to see you later."

"Why didn't she tell me herself?" she asked quizzically.

"She thinks that she did!" Christine answered.

She wheeled Suzie directly into the first examination room as her mom followed. She was to be the only patient today as May had calculated the importance of this exam and cleared the entire day's schedule. It wasn't hard; they didn't have a lot of patients yet, but word was getting around and the practice was growing. May had the unique ability to anticipate and prepare for almost anything, while Christine was always ready for whatever came up. The two were more than a team; they were extraordinarily competent.

Christine was taking Suzie's vitals when Thomas entered the room. Suzie's eyes sparkled and as she smiled, she began to cry.

"Well, don't cry!" the doctor spoke.

"I'm just too happy," she explained.

The doctor gave her a complete physical and listened to her heart over and over. "Would you step outside with me, Chris?" he asked. They left, but he quickly returned and continued to give her tests. She was weak, but in general she was very strong for what she had been through, he thought. Everything else about her was normal and strong. She was slightly underweight, but not much. She hadn't had infections; her sinus and lungs were normal. There was no sign of jaundice and she could breathe normally. It was her heart that caused her problems. It was only her heart.

Thomas turned to Isabel and said, "You have taken very good care of her, and it shows. One could expect many different complications from this condition if not for excellent care. I must commend you."

"Thank you!" she replied. "Melvin helps a lot too. She is very good at receiving care and taking her medicine too."

"Can you help me?" Suzie spoke up.

"We'll see," he answered.

Christine came back in and gave Suzie a coloring book and crayons and handed a magazine to her mom. Suzie quickly rolled onto her side and began to color as the doctor and his assistant left the room.

"Did you get the records?" he asked.

"Yes, and all the previous test results too. I ordered them yesterday knowing you would want to see them."

"Of course you did." He chuckled.

He looked over the test results and previous x-rays. Some very good doctors had examined her, and none could help her, and he was starting to understand why. He continued studying the charts and turned to Christine.

"Have them schedule an immediate set of heart X-rays. Be sure to specify we'll need anterior, posterior, and a lateral view." With that, he returned to the examination room, explained to them that someone was coming to get her for x-rays, then sat down at the desk. He sat there quietly studying her chart. After a while, he looked up to see Suzie smiling and drawing. She was studying him, then her paper as she drew him sitting at the desk. She had found the last page of the coloring book to be empty and was using that for her portrait. Isabel was not reading the magazine that he had brought her. Instead, she was sewing. She had brought her large purse and it was filled with garments that needed sewing repair.

"Is that what you do, sew?" he asked.

"Yes," she explained, "I take in all the sewing jobs from the cleaners downtown and people often bring me cloth that needs repair. I've been sewing most all of my life," she explained, "my grandmother taught me."

The doctor watched her intently as they talked. She sewed tiny stitches and she sewed them quickly. Each stitch was close to the last one and they were all exactly the same tension. The stitches were almost invisible as was the repair when she was finished. She was most certainly an expert seamstress.

"Your work is beautiful," he commented. "Did your grandmother teach you that stitch you're doing right now?"

"Yes and no," she replied. "She tried to teach me the stitch, but I could never quite get it, so I do it this way. I double wrap the thread and sew it from the back to the front. She always scoffed at me but I think it's easier and faster than her way."

They were interrupted by the orderly bringing in a gurney for the x-rays. Suzie smiled as it was again her new friend from the car. He smiled at her and, without a word, scooped her up and laid her down on the gurney.

"Mom will have to wait here, but I will stay with you the whole time, is that okay, Suzie?" the orderly explained.

"If you stay with me then okay," she answered.

With that, they were off and the two of them returned to their respective tasks.

Neither spoke a word for quite a while until Thomas broke the silence.

"How do you keep all the stitches the same tension? Is it because of all your experience?" he queried.

"Oh, not at all, come over and look closely, watch as I pull it tight. I can only pull it until it reaches the distance to the last stitch, I can't pull and squinch it all up. It's tight when it's pulled to the last stitch, and watch, because of the double wrap, it won't come loose at all. It's a hard stitch to learn but very easy to master."

"I see," the doctor replied as the door swung open and the orderly returned with Suzie. "You might as well help her to her wheelchair and prepare to take her home now. That will be enough poking and prodding for one day. Just what is your name, young man?" the doctor inquired.

"Frank, my name is Frank, Doctor Thomas," he answered.

"Good, I'll be sure to ask for you anytime Suzie needs to come in, would that be okay with you?"

"Oh yes, it would be just fine if you call for me to help Suzie. I would be happy to do that for you and for her."

"Well, that's settled then," he finished, as Suzie let out a big smile.

Frank wheeled her to the elevator with Isabel following. The doctor returned to his office and saw that Christine had already delivered a stack of papers. He started to read these papers as he waited for the new x-rays to be delivered.

Once home, Suzie was again lying in her bed when she called out, "Mom? Mom? Can you come here for a minute?"

Isabel went quickly to Suzie's room. "What is it?" she asked.

"Do you remember what Doctor Thomas said? Mom, do you?"

"Yes, but he said a lot of things, Suzie."

"Yes, but he said, we'll see. He said, we'll see, isn't that great, Mom?"

"Yes, dear, we'll see is a very encouraging answer. We'll see has hope built right into it, now doesn't it!"

"Oh yes, Mom, I'm so glad you heard it too." With that said, Suzie returned to her drawing and Isabel to her sewing.

# Chapter 4

## A Promotion

May's meeting with Julia did not go well. Julia explained that the hospital board had decided that they wanted to appoint Doctor Betterman as the head doctor for the hospital clinic. It was an unusual choice to pick such a young doctor, but the members had been evaluating him ever since he was a young intern. They were sure of their decision and wished to offer him the position before he established his own practice.

Julia explained, "We have a position to offer to you, if you would like it, in the maternity wing, but there is no open position for your sister Christine. They will want an answer right away. This will become a formal request Wednesday, but I felt I owed you the heads-up as I helped you get the secretary job for him. So, there you go. Do what you wish with the information, it's an open secret right now anyway."

May's mind was racing as she hurried back up to the office. She was not prepared for this news, and was in a position that was rare for her. May was confused. Thomas and Christine were still there studying the new x-rays in Thomas's office when May burst in.

"Julia has just leaked some important news to me," May announced. "She confided in me that Doctor Thomas Betterman has been chosen as the new head of the entire clinic and head surgeon there."

Thomas smiled and replied, "Really!"

"Yes," she answered, "really!"

"That would be highly unusual," he stammered. "Are you positive?"

"I'm absolutely positive. You don't know this, but Julia and I were roommates in college. I trust her implicitly."

"You're right, I didn't know that," he continued. "When was I to find out?"

"Wednesday," she answered.

"And the practice? And my office? And you girls? What is to become of all those things?"

"You would have to give up your practice, that's why they decided to offer you the position so soon. They wanted to offer it to you before you got your practice set up. I will be offered a good job in maternity, but they do not have any openings for Chris."

There was a long, quiet pause before Christine spoke. "I'll be just fine. I won't say I'm happy about it, but I do not want your decision based on me or my loss of a job. This is an outstanding opportunity for you and you can't let me be the one to affect it."

"I'm sorry, Chris," he spoke, "but you already have. May? You said they wanted to offer me the job before I got set up, correct?"

"Yes, that's what Julia said to me."

"Well, they are too late. Both of you go home tonight knowing that nothing in our plans or schedules will change! You girls have worked so hard and so well together, that we have already established the practice. We have patients scheduled for the rest of the week, and we have one patient in particular that we are not going to give up on. No, we will not give up for money or prestige. We are proceeding as planned."

"But doctor," May interrupted, "the salary alone, and the status? Are you sure?"

"May, Chris, I will accept the status and the prestige only after I deserve it in your eyes, only after I deserve it in Isabel's eyes, and only after I deserve it in the people of Hope's eyes. Not when it is only in the eyes of the hospital boardroom members. I've made my decision."

Christine spoke, and May noddingly agreed. "You are off to a great start." With that said, they went home for the night.

Thomas went home as well. While he lay there before sleep, he devised his plan.

On Wednesday, he was indeed called to the board meeting and they proposed their offer to him. Doctor Thomas was prepared. He stood up and greeted them all by name. "I am extremely humbled by your exciting offer and I wish for you to know that I am already aware of the promotion. I have known of this meeting for a few days and I have come to a hard-fought decision. Because I've already assembled a world-class staff and because of their proficiency, I already have numerous patients scheduled and one patient in particular that will exhaust most of my free time, I humbly must turn down your exceptional offer. I will, after careful thought, make a counteroffer. I will offer to take one clinic patient every weekday into my practice, free of charge. I will also come into the hospital every Saturday morning and make rounds in the clinic for free. I offer this to the hospital to repay all the opportunity that Hope Children's Hospital has given me."

Doctor Thomas received the answer the next day. They had accepted his offer. He then explained the deal he had made to both May and Christine.

# The Promise in a Brown Paper Bag

# Chapter 5

## Saturday Rounds

Thomas got up early Saturday morning and prepared for his new responsibility at the hospital. Although he had gone on rounds many times as an intern, this would be the first time it was his sole responsibility. He glanced at Suzie's window as he went to the bus stop, noting that she was not there to wave. Once he arrived, he was preparing for the rounds when the twin sisters entered the hospital.

"What are you two doing here on Saturday?" he asked.

"Did you think we would let you have all the fun?" Christine replied.

"We're here to help you," May added. "We're a team, right?"

The young doctor smiled at them and explained that he was about to determine where he was going to start out and the order and room numbers of the children he needed to visit.

"No problem," May replied. "I made the list last night after closing the office."

"And I have all the charts!" Christine added.

"Excellent," the doctor replied. "You two are something else!"

They started the rounds, meeting the children and some of their families. He liked the children and the children liked him. He told the parents to be sure to see him next Saturday if there were any problems that they encounter. The morning went by quickly, and by noon they were finished.

"Thank you, both of you, you two will make all the difference to these children. We really are going to do some good here. These families are used to a steady change in doctors and interns; a steady doctor and staff will make a big difference in their care, even if it is on Saturdays."

"You're right, Doctor Thomas," they answered in unison. "We're happy to help and do our part."

Thomas got off the bus and as he walked, he hoped to see Suzie waving. As he reached her house, he was happy to see her waving in the window. He waved back, went up and knocked at the door. Isabel greeted him warmly. He told her he wanted to see Suzie at the office on Tuesday and would send Frank to get them. She nodded and showed him to

Suzie's room. Suzie beamed a smile when she saw him. For the first time, she didn't cry; she just smiled and reached out her arms. The good doctor gave her a gentle hug and knelt beside her bed as she showed him the pictures she had drawn. It was hard to believe, but her drawings seemed to be getting better even during this short time.

"Your pictures are all very good!" he exclaimed. "They seem to be improving at a rapid pace!"

Suzie explained, "Melvin brought me a library book home from school. I have been using it to help me. I can't wait until I can go to school too!"

"That was very nice of him," the doctor said as he bid her goodbye and approached Isabel.

"I will see you Tuesday, okay?" he asked.

"Of course, Thomas, thank you, thank you very much for all you do for us."

"Do me a favor, will you?" he asked. "Bring some sewing work in with you, if you don't mind. There's something I want to discuss with you while we wait."

"Sure, I always have sewing work to do. That will be no problem," she answered while wondering what he wanted to discuss.

"It's not important," he said as he left. Once on the street, he counted the seven steps back to Suzie's window and smiled as she was there waving. He waved goodbye and continued his walk home.

Thomas didn't mind having to go to the hospital on Saturdays. He really didn't have much to do on weekends anyway. He usually spent weekends reading and studying. He loved to read, so he was not lonely, but he spent way too much time on the weekends alone. Even seeing Suzie and Isabel was an unusual event in his normal routine and brought a smile to his face. I enjoy my reading and solitude, he thought. I'm not lonely, he convinced himself.

The rest of his weekend he spent reading and studying what he learned about Suzie's heart condition. He made a note for May of some of the heart experts that he wanted to consult with. He also made a list of some papers that were published on the subject, and information that Christine could compile and study with him. It was late Sunday night as Thomas readied himself for bed, when he picked up a silly spy, detective, and mystery novel he had been reading. He read one chapter, as always, to take his mind off work and fall quickly to sleep.

# Chapter 6

## Diagnosis

Monday morning was quiet as they only had one patient and one patient from the clinic. The boy from the clinic had croup, and the doctor gave him a dose of dexamethasone and sent him home to recover. The rest of the day was spent making calls to consult with other doctors and specialists about Suzie's heart condition. They were all helpful and offered advice, but none had either tried or succeeded in performing a transposition of the great arteries, none except the last name on the list. Dr. Paola had been successful in his last six attempts at switching the pulmonary artery and aorta. The catch was, they were all under two years old.

"It would be very hard to successfully do the operation on a seven-year-old," Dr. Paola explained. "The arteries are much bigger, and it takes more time to stitch the arteries back together. The main concern is time. After cooling the body to reach hypothermia, you do not have time to switch and sew the arteries properly. The younger the children are, the longer time you can have them in hypothermia and that they can withstand and recover. At seven, it's just too much. I hate to inform you of this, but you have already passed your window of opportunity."

Doctor Thomas asked Dr. Paola if they could consult again if he learned any advancements. He agreed and told Thomas that he would await his call.

Tuesday morning saw Frank once again wheel Suzie into the examination room.

# The Promise in a Brown Paper Bag

Frank carried her to the examination table and squeezed her hand. Suzie smiled and lay there awaiting the tests. Christine came in and took her vitals, followed closely by the doctor. Christine prepared her chest with a gel and started the ultrasound exam. The doctor watched closely and confirmed his suspicion. He then asked Suzie to sit up, helping her as she sat up for him. He then told her to lie back and do it again. Carefully, he helped her to lay back down again.

"Lie there quietly please, Suzie, can you do that for me?"

"Okay," she replied, obviously winded.

"Frank? After she calms back down, will you take her down to the cafeteria and get her any ice cream that she wants, okay?"

"Sure thing, Doc! Anything you say!" he answered.

A short time later, Frank took Suzie, and the doctor approached Isabel, quietly sewing in the corner.

"I would like you to teach me that invisible stitch that you showed me last time we talked. You know, that one your grandmother tried to teach you, but that instead you improved?"

"Well sure, I will be glad to teach you, but what makes you so interested in my sewing?" she asked.

"Your stitch could be instrumental in saving Suzie's life," he explained. "Let me explain." The doctor paused as he tried to figure out how to tell her in layman's terms.

"Suzie has Transposition of the Great Arteries. That just means the main arteries connected to her heart are connected backwards. In an operation, I will have to cut them both and sew them back to where the other was and vice versa. Right now, in her heart, the oxygen-rich blood is getting pumped right back into her lungs and the oxygen-poor blood is being pumped through her body. She also has a slight anomaly that would be okay if her heart pumped normally, but since it's not pumping normally, it's actually the thing that has kept her alive. You see, her heart has a slight leak between the chambers, and oxygen-rich blood leaks into the other chamber, mixing with the oxygen-poor blood. It's not enough, but it has been enough to keep her alive. I've just confirmed with this last test that when her heart starts to beat faster, the leak is almost nonexistent, and the more her body needs oxygen, the less it can get. You must redouble your efforts to keep her calm until I can come up with a way to save her."

"And my stitch?" she asked.

"Yes, your stitch is much faster than my normal suture, a great deal faster! If I can learn your stitch and sew her arteries without it coming loose or pulling too tight, if I don't have to tie off my stitch each time, if I can start and finish using the same suture the entire way around the artery, I just might be able to do it fast enough so Suzie can survive the operation."

"Well then, of course I will teach you. You stop at the house anytime you walk by and I will teach you whatever you need to learn," she answered, happy to help.

That is exactly what Thomas did. The very next time he walked home from the hospital, he stopped at Suzie's house and Isabel showed him how to sew. He stopped for about an hour every night for the next two weeks. He would bring a drawing book or some drawing supplies, and Suzie would sit at the table drawing them as they sewed together. Isabel would always make him a bite to eat and drink. She enjoyed this time together, and his interest in the stitch made her feel more important and prouder that she was helping Suzie get better.

These two weeks were more than he needed; with her instruction, he had gotten very good at sewing two pieces of cloth together. Soon he was sewing almost as fast and as precise as Isabel.

One evening as he finished sewing some scraps together, he held the patch up to the light and pulled the pieces apart.

Try as he might, he could not see any light passing through the patch.

"Cut one of the threads for me, Isabel. I want to see what happens if a stitch breaks."

Isabel took the small shears and carefully cut a thread in his patch. He continued pulling, but holding it to the light, he could not find the broken stitch.

"Cut a few more, spacing them out as I pull. Okay?" he asked. She proceeded to cut the patch three more times, spacing the cuts out evenly.

"Nothing," he declared, "I cannot see the breaks! Cut again, please, but cut two or three stitches in a row."

Isabel cut the stitches as he pulled the piece apart until finally, he saw where she was cutting. He continued to pull after she finished and pulled even harder. He could see a small opening, but he could not make it worse.

"This will work even better than I thought," he explained, "thank you so much for teaching me and for all your time."

"It has been my pleasure," she replied. "Stop in anytime; you are always welcome here."

Doctor Thomas left the house knowing that he would miss these evenings. This had been the closest thing to a family that he had experienced in a long time. He started for home but again stopped and backed up the seven steps to wave goodbye to Suzie.

# The Promise in a Brown Paper Bag

# Chapter 7

## It's Time

Doctor Thomas continued to practice. He had bought some soft rubber tubing for practice. Once proficient with the tubing, he moved on to cadavers at the morgue. With Christine assisting, he had gotten his time down to eight and a half minutes. He was ready to call Dr. Paola again.

The conversation with Dr. Paola turned bleak again. "You have gotten your time to a point of probability of success, but you have no room for error," he explained. "You need to be able to do this even faster. Call me again when you can perform the reattachments quicker than even eight minutes."

Christine and May were both in his office listening to the conversation on speakerphone. Their faces were in dismay. They sat there in silence until Christine spoke up.

"I have an idea!" she exclaimed. "I've watched you many times, and when you sew the outside of the artery on the backside it slows you way down."

"What is your idea?" Thomas asked.

"What if you didn't sew the backside of the artery on the outside, but instead sewed it on the inside? You would start by sewing on the inside at the spot it usually gets harder, and switch to sewing on the outside to finish the repair. You should be able to sew as fast as possible the entire procedure. You would only need to learn a stitch to join the stitches at the reversal and the ending."

The doctor sat there in awe. It was a simple idea, but he realized it could work. If it works, this would cut the time significantly. Soon they were back at the morgue, and his new times were smashing his old fastest record. He was at six and a half minutes, even with going back and using the original single stitching method to hold the four spots he had transitioned from back to front.

"I'm almost ready!" Both girls were now with him, as May had decided to assist her sister. She wanted to be a part of this procedure and was ready to do her part. "I'm going to ask Isabel if she can devise a transition stitch to eliminate the need for the four stitches at the end. If she can do that, I will call Dr. Paola again and ask him to come to my hospital and supervise the heart procedure."

Walking home, he saw the light was still on in the kitchen of Isabel's house. It was late, but he was anxious to speak with her, so he knocked. Isabel answered the door. She looked tired, but she welcomed him in.

"What brings the Doctor around at this time of night? It must be important?" Isabel spoke.

Thomas explained the problem to her, and she picked up one of his pieces of rubber hose. She fumbled with it as she sewed the stitches and transitioned from the inside to the outside. She had tried a dozen times before she smiled and said, "Here, try this cross stitch."

Thomas looked at it, and she slowly showed him the transitioning stitch. It was almost too easy. It was a simple X stitch that ended ready to sew on the outside. At the end, he would tie it off and be done. It took seconds and eliminated more than a minute.

"Perfect!" he exclaimed. "You are truly an expert seamstress."

The stitch was so simple he didn't need to practice it. He would call Dr. Paola in the morning, hoping he would decide to come and supervise the operation. He then read from his book to blot out all the thoughts of the busy day and went to sleep.

The next morning May again connected Doctor Thomas to Dr. Paola. Thomas explained the ideas Christine had offered and the improvements in time. He also explained the transition stitch. Dr. Paola listened intently and agreed to come supervise the surgery as long as The Hope Children's Hospital board approved the surgery and Thomas would teach him the stitches.

Thomas declined the offer. To be clear, he only declined the part where he would teach the stitch to Dr. Paola. "I will not teach you the stitches," he retorted, "but I will introduce you to Isabel, the one that invented the stitch, and I'm sure she will teach it to you for a price for her time and invention."

Dr. Paola laughed out loud. "Of course, of course," he repeated, "the innovator should always be rewarded for their invention! I am even a bigger fan of yours for your stand. Trust that I too will act the same, only pointing my colleagues to this Isabel to learn her technique also."

With that settled, all they could do was wait for the board's decision to allow the innovative surgery.

# Chapter 8

## The Operation

The Hope Children's Hospital Board of Directors presented their findings early the next week. They had approved the innovative operation with an agreement that Dr. Paola, the distinguished surgeon from Brazil, would be the lead doctor and Dr. Thomas Betterman would assist.

The initial happiness and celebration soon became somber as they remembered that Suzie's life was on the line. The smiles soon came back to them all as they realized, that with Dr. Paola's help, success was imminent.

May scheduled the operation for Saturday, after rounds. Dr. Paola was to fly in on Friday for a meet-and-greet and inspection of the operating room and equipment. May also scheduled an appointment with Isabel to teach him the stitches if after the surgery he still wanted to learn.

On Saturday, Dr. Paola was ready as Thomas finished talking to Suzie, and prepared for the operation. Suzie had been the first and the last patient he saw that morning. Frank and her mom were with her now waiting outside. Once they were ready, Frank brought Suzie into the operating room and helped her onto the operating table. He then retreated to the corner, refusing to leave her as he had promised.

Soon she was asleep and they cooled her body down. Dr. Paola opened her chest with a sternal saw, and his assistant quickly inserted the sternal retractors and separated her chest and ribs. They watched as the chilled body reached hypothermia and her heart slowed then stopped. Dr. Paola was ready and quickly snipped the two main arteries, then stepped back. Doctor Thomas took over and quickly attached the aorta to its proper ventricle on the heart. He started sewing with the inside stitch and was about to make the transition stitch when it happened. He dropped the needle.

Christine quickly retrieved it with her forceps. May took the moment and reached out and dried his glove; she wiped his brow as he resumed sewing.

Dr. Paola's voice boomed, "Compose yourself and continue your work, everything will be fine. We have factored small mishaps into our plan."

Thomas continued to sew faster and with even more precision. May wiped his brow again and again as he concentrated. He started the other artery and was in a rhythm as he sewed it into place, and then he was done. As quickly as it had started, it was now over.

Dr. Paola studied the stitches as they warmed her body. "Exquisite," he said. "That is beautiful work, my good friend."

Doctor Thomas reached into her chest and massaged her heart and it started beating. It was beating strong and there was no sign of a leak. Even the transition stitches were holding fine. Dr. Paola gave another quick look and his assistant and Christine worked together to close the chest and stitch her back up.

Frank wheeled her to the recovery room, only leaving her side to get Isabel. They sat there together waiting for her to resume consciousness as Isabel continued to get up and kiss her forehead and feel her hand.

"She's too cold!" her mom kept repeating.

Frank had to reassure her each time that she would be alright and that everything went just fine. "She'll be fine," Frank reminded her. "That's normal; she was in hypothermia for the last hour. It's normal for her to feel cold. She will slowly warm back up. Do not worry."

They were sitting there when both teams poured into the recovery room. Everyone was excited to see her awaken. Christine recorded her vital signs while Dr. Paola and his assistant checked her pupils. Everything was within the normal range.

After a short wait, Suzie started to stir. She opened her eyes to see Doctor Thomas on one side and her mother on the other. "Where is the doctor?" she asked Thomas.

"I'm right here, I'm your doctor, Suzie. Your operation is all over now."

"But where's my mom?" she asked frantically.

"I'm right here too," said Isabel as she reached out and held her hand.

"Oh. Good," Suzie said, "I thought you got lost!"

"Lost? No, I didn't get lost, I've just been waiting for you this whole time."

Suzie looked around and went right back to sleep.

She woke up again a few minutes later not realizing she had slept.

"I have a boyfriend, you know," she proudly said. Both her mom and Thomas said they didn't know that. "He's Frank's, where is Frank?"

"I'm right here!" said Frank as he stood up at the bottom of her bed.

"Yes, of course you are, Frank always stays with me when I'm scared. Frank has a brother that's my age! His name is Billy," she proclaimed, "and he said he likes me! Silly boy, he hasn't ever even seen me. What if I turn out to be ugly? Then what's he going to say?"

"You are not ugly; you are very pretty," Mom stated.

"But what if I turn ugly, like the ugly duckling?"

"The ugly duckling turned into a beautiful swan, dear. It was not ugly. You already turned into a beautiful young girl. You turned out just fine, and with Doctor Thomas's help and care, you will make some boy an excellent girlfriend."

"That's good to know, yes, I'll have to remember that," Suzie replied and fell right back to sleep.

Isabel looked at the two doctors standing there. "Is she going to be alright? Is she going to be normal, is she saved?"

Doctor Thomas looked at her and said, "We'll see."

She then looked at Dr. Paola and he said, "Yes, we have to wait and see, but all indications so far are very good."

And so, they waited. They kept her in bed and tried to keep her calm. They gave her an endless supply of art supplies and got her anything to eat that she wanted. She was not gaining weight, but she was getting stronger. During her second week in the hospital, nurses noticed that she was staying in bed, but moving around on the bed often. She would be coloring, then change to drawing at the bottom of the bed, then she would be sitting on the edge reading a book. Isabel and Frank noticed the changes too. Soon, everyone agreed, Suzie was getting better. Doctor

Thomas would smile seeing the improvement, and Frank would torment her about the crazy things she said in the recovery room.

Finally, the doctor gave permission for her to get out of bed and take short walks assisted by the nurses or Frank. Suzie was ready to go.

"Easy, easy, slow down!" Frank would say. "Baby steps!" as she tried to hurry ahead. Frank knew that the operation was a success and that she would soon be running around playing like his younger brother or any other kid her age. Everyone, including Frank, was just trying to make sure her recovery and healing went well, and so far, it had. Doctor Thomas took note of Frank's efforts to help Suzie recover and recommended him for a position in the new program to train physical therapists. Frank would be perfect for that job, he thought.

It was one month to the day when Dr. Thomas signed the orders that she could be released to go home. Her recovery wasn't over, but he trusted Isabel to keep her reined in and provide a recovery regimen. He also planned to stop in and see her often, if not every night after work.

Christine had kept in touch with Dr. Paola's assistant and kept them informed of Suzie's progress for the duration of her stay. She now let them know of her pending release. Thomas and Dr. Paola spoke often and agreed to continue to consult on these operations; the Brazilian doctor had learned the stitching from Isabel and had convinced his hospital, the Instituto Dante Pazzanese de Cardiologia, to set up an endowment to cover any costs of Suzie's education.

# Chapter 9

## The Brown Paper Bag

Suzie was all packed up and waiting for Frank to take her and her mom home. She should have been happy, but instead she was sad, and when Doctor Thomas came in to bid her goodbye, she started crying.

"Why are you crying?" he asked.

"I'm just so sad that we cannot afford the huge bill that my mom got in the mail," she cried.

"Well now don't," he started to say, but Suzie interrupted.

"I thought up an idea on how I can repay you," she explained.

"What is your idea?" the doctor asked.

Suzie reached behind her back and pulled out a brown paper bag. "I will give you this bag, and the promise to put things in it for you."

"What will you put in it?" he asked.

"We'll see," she answered.

And with that, he accepted the paper bag as payment.

Frank came and picked them up to take them home, and the doctor continued his rounds. For the rest of the afternoon, all he could think was, 'we'll see.'

The doctor finished his rounds, said goodbye to the twins, and took the bus home as usual. Walking up the street, he noticed the change. Suzie was outside waiting for him. He greeted her and gave her a hug while walking her back to the house, he greeted Isabel and said goodbye. He started to walk home but took the seven steps backwards only to see Suzie already in the window and waving. He smiled and waved and proceeded home. Once he reached the porch, he carefully unfolded the brown paper bag and positioned it next to his favorite outdoor chair. He retrieved a rock from the garden and placed it inside the bag to keep the wind from blowing it away. Sitting down beside the bag, his mind wandered. What would she put in the bag? He drew a complete blank. He had no idea what was in her mind to put in the bag.

The summer days passed and one particularly nice day, he walked past and waved at Suzie, and as he approached his house, he noticed that something was sticking out of the bag. He hurried up to it and found it to be full of sweet corn. He sat there smiling and shucking corn. Day after day it was filled with corn. Corn was overflowing, and he had eaten his fill every night. The doctor had more corn than he knew what to do with, so he called a poor family that also lived on the street and gave some to them. He took corn to work and insisted the twins take it home. He offered the corn to anyone that would listen.

He was almost happy when he saw the corn was not overflowing the bag one nice evening. But when he looked down inside, he found it full of tomatoes. The next day it was zucchini. Then carrots, after that onions, broccoli, and cauliflower. One garden treat after another, the doctor always had a full refrigerator of fresh garden vegetables.

As fall set in, the bag was not filled as often, with the exception of some squash, pumpkins, and a watermelon. He was just about sure that the bag, now well-worn, had come to its end, but he was wrong. Another relative had an orchard, and the bag was soon filled with apples. Later it was full of pears, then plums, then cherries. Oranges and peaches soon appeared in the bag. The doctor had a great amount of fun, eating and sharing the contents of the paper bag.

Winter was coming, and the wind was starting to blow cold. The doctor shuffled up the street, waving to Suzie and hurrying home, stopping only to glance inside the bag. Inside was a warm pair of slippers. What a beautiful gesture, he thought, going inside and trying them on. They fit perfectly and were very warm. The doctor was aglow with happiness. The next day the bag produced a pipe and some tobacco. He went inside, put on his heavy winter coat and his warm slippers, and then went back outside and sat in his chair beside the brown paper bag. He gazed at Suzie and Isabel's house as he puffed on his new pipe. It was that moment when Thomas realized that this brown paper bag was the best payment for a debt that he would ever receive.

# Chapter 10

## Toys

The bag continued to be filled every once in a while, that winter. A pair of gloves, some magazines, gum, and an invitation for dinner on Friday night were some of the things that showed up in the brown bag. Thomas took advantage of the invite and showed up after work to a nice home-cooked meal. Suzie and Melvin were extremely helpful and made the doctor extra welcome, and they enjoyed the meal. They sat there afterwards and Suzie showed him all her new drawings, carefully remembering all the pictures he seemed to like best. Those would go into the bag, she decided. Melvin showed him his new toys and shirt. He was happy that he got some new clothes for school. Isabel had come into some extra money after teaching the two doctors that came to learn the stitch. They were quite impressed and generous in paying her for her time. She explained that she had two more doctors scheduled, and many more had shown interest. The doctor agreed to help her if she decided to set up a studio and wanted to teach her sewing instead of actually doing all the sewing. Isabel was tickled with the idea.

"You be sure to stop next Friday for dinner again, that is if you like our company," she offered.

He did, and he did. In fact, he started to stop for dinner every Friday. It became a weekly ritual and Thomas always looked forward to the gracious meal. He also noticed that over the passing year, the dinner had become much more elaborate. There were plenty of fruits and vegetables, of course, and his bag continued to be overflowing with them too, but the entire meal was improved, and the kitchen, and the dinnerware. Everything was being improved, not just the food. Isabel had become prosperous due to teaching her stitch.

On one of the Friday meals, Isabel informed the doctor that she had heard about a boutique in town that had closed its doors, and that the shop was up for rental. They discussed the idea at length and had soon agreed that she should make the switch from sewing to teaching. She would be able to have both students and more time for the many surgeons wanting to come to Hope and learn her unusual stitch. Thomas, true to his word, agreed to help.

Thomas called Christine to help, Christine called May, and May called Julia. The three girls, working with Isabel, made short work of the contracts, negotiations, and the paperwork needed to take over the shop. They coordinated the efforts to remodel and transform the store into a first-rate sewing school. Their work was impressive, and soon Isabel's Stitches - School of Sewing was born.

It was an instant success. Doctors were coming to Hope to learn, and the local middle school sent class after class of Home Economics students to learn to sew. Soon the high school was sending students to earn Technical School credits for graduation.

Melvin was a big help after school, readying supplies and helping clean up. Suzie helped too, but mostly she could be found painting and drawing the building and the classrooms. They all loved being at, and spending their time at, the store. After two years of renting, Isabel bought the entire building. The building included a somewhat luxurious three-bedroom apartment, and they quickly made plans to move in.

It was a Thursday evening after work when Thomas walked past Suzie's house. He couldn't see Suzie's window as a large moving truck had parked right in front of it. The place was busy with workers moving furniture and boxes out of the house and into the truck. Doctor Thomas allowed himself to be sad. Just for a bit, he thought. I will miss my friends badly, and it will have a strong impact. It would be normal to be sad.

The next day he stopped in front of Suzie's window. It was empty, of course. The front door was swinging back and forth open to the squirrels and flies. It wasn't much of a house to begin with; it was just a shack. He realized that it would not even be here for long, erasing his memories and the sadness in his heart. He continued home and noticed something in the bag. It was a Happy Meal from McDonald's. He smiled and broke his sadness. As he ate, he fished the small toy out of the bag. It was a small rocket ship of sorts and opened to a little man driving. I'll save this on my bookshelf, he thought, examining it as if it was a prize. The meal and the toy were important as it meant that they too were thinking about him.

The years passed quickly, two then four then six as the doctor continued his normal schedule. The bag was filled less often, but at harvest he always had fresh vegetables and fruit. This bag keeps me eating healthy, he mused.

On the other hand, Isabel was prospering. She was bringing in and teaching between five and six doctors and surgeons from around the world, every week. They would bring their families and stay at the nearby hotel. For the most part, they were wealthy and toured the nearby businesses and eating establishments. The whole community felt the benefits of her sewing business. Business in the neighborhood was booming, and she became friends with many of the nearby business owners. The increase in business was so noticeable that the Hope Chamber of Commerce awarded her school 'The Most Promising New Business' award, and at the ceremony the mayor gave her the 'Key to the City.'

Isabel was happy. It showed in her smile. Her appearance improved with the years. She now patronized the local hairdresser, nail salon and beauty spa, and it showed. She had a new glow and she would get a hold of Suzie every once in a while, and hug and kiss her. Suzie would be embarrassed, especially around other people when she did this, but Isabel always remembered that it was Suzie that was both the anchor that weighed them into poverty, but also the hot air balloon that rose them up to prosperity.

Thomas walked up the street to his home. He glanced over to where Suzie's window used to stand and wave. The old shack was gone now. They had demolished it last spring, and it saddened him to walk past every day. He stopped, took and counted his steps as he walked backwards towards the spot where he used to wave at Suzie, and he waved anyway. During the rest of the walk home he realized why he had always done that. He realized that after the meal, after the sewing and after coming to see them, he always wanted to show her that she and she alone was the most important thing on his mind.

He continued walking and as he reached the porch he was amazed. The brown paper bag was overflowing with toys. Not only the bag, but there were boxes overflowing too. He examined the paper bag and on the very top were two small dolls, a boy doll and a girl doll. The doctor recognized them on first sight. These will go on my bookshelf, he decided. He placed them, using them as bookends on the shelf. He remembered Melvin pantomiming the dolls' routine, and Suzie saying I knew you would come, I always knew you would come. A tear came to his eye and he hurried back to the porch. What will I do with all these toys, he wondered. He looked over the contents, there were Happy Meal toys and matchbox cars, teddy bears and action figures. There were all kinds and types of toys for both boys and girls. All the toys from Suzie's and Melvin's youth were in and around the brown paper bag.

Thomas took the toys inside and sorted them into piles. He decided to take them to the hospital and give them to all the children. Every Saturday after that, he filled his pockets with toys before he went to work.

That Saturday, Doctor Thomas, Christine, and May went into the first young clinic patient's room. They examined the boy and talked to him and his mom. They checked his chart and made the necessary changes before saying goodbye and leaving. It was then, after they had all left, that the doctor walked the seven steps backwards back into the room. He presented the young boy with a present from inside his pocket, smiled and waved goodbye.

That became his new routine. He would always walk backwards back into the room and give them a toy and a wave to assure the child that they were important to him. It worked like a charm.

It didn't take long for the nurses and doctors to discover how popular he was with the children. They were amazed at the fact that he only worked Saturdays and had become so popular. The Hospital administrator also found out and had Julia write some letters of recommendation for his behavior and present them to the board for approval. The board approved, and Julia sent them right out to all the physician and surgeon oversight and award committees. She also nominated both May and Christine for the hospital's highest award.

In the months that followed, May won the Hope Children's Hospital 'Secretary of the Year' award. It was soon followed by the 'Nurse of the Year' award for Christine. They displayed their awards proudly and wondered if the doctor had been noticed. Their answer came shortly as Doctor Thomas Betterman soon won the American College of Surgeons 'Distinguished Service' award, and the Royal College of Surgeons 'Gold Medal.'

It was later that month when Thomas got a call to go to the White House for a meeting with the President of the United States. During the meeting, the President awarded him the 'Presidential Medal of Freedom.'

During the coming months, Julia became the new Hospital Administrator as her boss accepted the role of Chairman of the Board. May was picked as her new assistant and Christine became the head nurse at the hospital. Doctor Thomas quickly accepted the prestigious job as Head Surgeon for both the Hope Children's Hospital and the Hope Children's Clinic. All of the awards, promotions, and prestige were the direct result from a brown paper bag filled with toys.

"There can be no greater gift in the bag than those toys," the doctor proclaimed, but he was wrong. He was very wrong.

# The Promise in a Brown Paper Bag

# Chapter 11

## The Gift

It was a beautiful spring Saturday morning, and Thomas was sitting on the porch next to the empty bag. It was very old and torn. It had stains and a hole. Thomas was about to finally throw it away. Suzie was off at art school, and Isabel and Melvin were busy at the school, so the old brown paper bag had not been used in a while. Desperate to cling to the bygone days, he changed his mind and got some masking tape. He taped up the rips and patched the hole. He then placed the entire old bag inside a new one. Good as new, he thought. I'll leave it here as a reminder even though it will probably never be filled again. That is where he was wrong.

One spring morning, while walking back home after work, Thomas was about the spot where the old shack was at, when he noticed the paper bag on the porch blowing in the wind. That would not have been unusual, except it was one of the most calm, windless days that Hope had experienced in a long time. He stopped and watched as it was motionless. Perhaps I imagined it, he thought as he continued his walk. As he got closer, the brown paper bag wiggled again and the doctor ran up and looked down into the bag. His mouth was wide open and his eyes the size of saucers.

Suzie was actually home from art school on spring break. She called Frank at the hospital.

"Hello? Frank? It's Suzie."

"Well hello, Suzie, long time no see!" he answered. "What brings you to call me? At work even? Is it important?"

"Yes, I think it's very important," Suzie explained. "Can you come get me at my mom's school and take me somewhere after you are done working?"

"Sure!" Frank answered. "It will be fun seeing you again. Where are we going?"

"I'll explain later," she told him. "By the way, where is your brother William?"

"Oh, Billy? He's around somewhere. Why? What's up?" Frank asked.

"No, I mean where is he right now?"

"Home, I suppose," Frank thought about it. "I'm not sure, but he was at home this morning when I left."

"Oh, okay, never mind then," Suzie said with a hint of sadness in her voice.

"He's been home on spring break most of the week. Why ask?" Frank inquired.

"Spring break?" Suzie repeated back. "Does he go to college?"

"Yeah, some art school in Seattle, Cornish?" Frank said.

"Cornish College of the Arts?" Suzie pressed Frank.

"Yeah, I think that's it. Why?" he wondered.

"Oh, I'm not crazy!" Suzie explained. "That's where I go to school too! I thought I saw him on campus, but I wasn't sure. I was too shy to approach him to find out. Okay, never mind about all that. Pick me up after work. We have something important to do."

"Okay, Suzie, it will be an adventure." Frank ended.

Frank picked Suzie up after work. He would have brought Billy but he was nowhere to be found. Probably off playing pool somewhere, Frank thought. Suzie got in and directed him to the local dog pound. The air at the pound was pungent, but they slowly checked every cage.

"He's not here," Suzie proclaimed.

"You're sure?" Frank asked.

"Positive!" she answered. "Let's go."

The next stop was a private dog rescue facility and it didn't take Suzie long before she said, "Sorry, he's just not here." Frank drove on and they stopped at a pet store. They had a great selection of very cute puppies. Suzie hugged and petted the little balls of fur, but again said that he wasn't there.

Frank drove to the last place on her list. It was in the country on the outskirts of

Hope. He stopped and read the sign: The Golden Tails Kennel. In smaller letters it said, Home of: International Champion Montgomery 'Sweet Pea' Goldentail, at Stud.

They entered the small office, and as they went in, an elderly lady yelled, "Sweetpea! Come here, someone wants to pet you." Sweet Pea trotted in and brushed up against Suzie. Indeed, she wanted to pet him. Frank stroked his soft fur and asked if she had any puppies for sale.

"Just one left," the lady explained, "but wait, I'll show you the mother. Pancake! You come too!" On cue, Pancake trotted out. Pancake was very well mannered. She sat there as they petted her and Sweetpea.

"Sweetpea is an American and Canadian Champion, but Pancake has never been showed," she explained. "She's a purebred Golden, and registered and all, but we never took her to the dog shows to compete."

"Okay, that's great, can we see the puppy?" Suzie asked.

"Of course you can. Come this way." She walked into the kennel and went to a room that looked more like a kid's playroom or old living room than a place for puppies. "He's been very lonely lately," she explained. "Being picked last and all."

Suzie stepped in and there he was, a tiny English Cream Golden Retriever puppy. Just a little ball of fur. The little puppy bounced over to her and she picked him up. He collapsed in her arms as if he knew she was there to save him.

"I can't save you, little guy," she told the puppy, "but I know someone that can." Frank knew that she had found what she was looking for, and they bought the puppy for the good doctor.

The good doctor regained his composure and reached into the brown bag and pulled out the puppy. The puppy squirmed and wiggled as the doctor sat down in his chair. The puppy nuzzled his face and wriggled up into his neck. The doctor then repositioned the little puppy in his lap and as if on cue, the puppy went to sleep. Thomas was sitting as still as he could, so as not to awaken the pup, when the car turned onto the street and approached the house. It parked in front of the house and Frank, Suzie, Isabel and Melvin got out. As they approached the porch, another car turned in, then another. May and her family, followed by Christine and her family, pulled up and parked.

Frank was carrying a large bag of puppy chow, while Suzie had a dog bed. Melvin held a collar, and May had a leash. Everyone had a present for the dog, but the last one out of the cars was Isabel, and she was carrying a large cake with forty candles burning brightly as she approached the porch. It was Thomas's birthday and Suzie had planned the whole thing.

Another car pulled onto the street. It raced up the street, the motor roaring, and William jumped out of the hot rod and yelled, "Am I too late?"

"Not at all," Suzie answered, and she went down, grabbed his hand and guided him up onto the porch, then into the large country kitchen. The cake was on the table along with the dog's bed. Suzie took the pup and placed it into the bed, but he just stood there looking at the burning candles. Everyone sang 'Happy Birthday' to Thomas and the lights went out. He blew the candles out in the dark, but it was the brightest moment that that old kitchen ever had.

The lights came back on and they cut and enjoyed the cake, all talking at once. William, or Billy as Frank still called him, was trying to get the puppy to come out of his bed and eat the cake. He took some icing and touched the puppy's nose. He licked it off but refused to create the ruckus that Billy so badly wanted to see.

"That's his name then, Billy, thank you for that," Thomas declared.

"What's his name?" Suzie pleaded.

"Well, he refuses to ruckus," Thomas answered. "So, his name will be Rufus!"

Everyone agreed that it was an excellent name and continued celebrating the doctor throughout the evening.

Rufus was the best thing that ever happened to the doctor. Thomas was not lonely ever again. Rufus grew and grew and he grew to be Thomas's best friend. They played and played. Thomas taught Rufus tricks and having Rufus taught Thomas many things over the years. They were inseparable, except for when the doctor went to work. When gone, Rufus would wait patiently on the porch and when he heard the bus coming, race down the street to meet his master. Together they would walk up the street to his house as he threw a stick for Rufus to chase or a ball for him to retrieve. For many, many days in a row, the doctor would forget about the old house and window. He would forget about waving to Suzie, he would forget about the grief from them moving. Instead, he would happily walk and run with Rufus, easily forgetting all his troubles and cares.

The doctor pondered the paper bag and determined that indeed Rufus was the best thing that could ever be in a brown paper bag. Although he was certain and thought that he could not possibly be wrong this time, there was still a lingering thought in his head. That thought was, "We'll see."

# Chapter 12

## The End

Suzie caught up to William one day on campus. She grabbed his hand and told him that he should buy his girlfriend lunch today, and he did. From that day on, they were inseparable. It was on graduation day that he proposed. She told him yes, and they planned a small wedding.

Her college roommate was her maid of honor, while Frank was the best man. Doctor Thomas stepped up as father of the bride and Isabel cried with joy. It turned out beautiful, and they honeymooned in the Bahamas. Suzie had not only survived her heart abnormality, she had excelled in everyone's eyes.

William taught art at the local college, and Suzie showed her work all over the world. Her paintings were accepted to be some of the best and her exhibitions were welcomed everywhere. Her art was coveted by some of the most avid collectors and her fame spread rapidly.

Suzie would join her husband at the school occasionally and help him with his open class for the community, and each time she was there the auditorium would be overflowing. Suzie was indeed a success in the art world.

The doctor continued to go to the hospital on Saturdays, even after he had retired. Old Rufus was finally allowed on the bus, and the doctor took him with him to help the children. Rufus followed the doctors all throughout the hospital meeting all the children. He would let them pet him, show off the many tricks that the doctor had taught him, and he would even get on the bed and lay beside some of the very sick patients. Rufus brought joy to the hearts of all the children that he encountered.

It wasn't long after Rufus was gone that the doctor found himself in the hospital. They gave the doctor a special room in the Hope Children's Hospital and he was visited by some of the best doctors from around the world.

"There's nothing I can say, Doctor Betterman," one such doctor said. "There is no cure."

"We can't help you," said another, "It's just not in our power."

Doctor after doctor came, and all were saying the same thing. They told him it was hopeless and that they couldn't say anything to make him happy.

Doctor Thomas replied to each one the same. "We'll see." Was all he would say.

Late one evening as the doctor was lying in bed, he had a visitor. It was none other than Suzie. The artist of great acclaim was standing beside his bed and he looked up to see her holding an old brown paper bag. It was falling apart as it was stuffed with pictures and paintings. The brown paper bag had been taped many times and had string tied around it to hold it together. She carefully handed him the overflowing bag.

"I hope this covers the full cost of my debt to you," she said, tears welling in her eyes. "This is the last time I will be able to fill up the bag."

The doctor carefully opened and looked at the first picture from the bag. It was a drawing she had made in her bedroom showing a handsome young doctor kneeling beside her bed. The next was the picture from the back of the coloring book, showing Doctor Thomas at the desk reading the charts and the exams. There were more pictures, lots more. There were pictures of him eating corn, lots of pictures of the corn. There were pictures of the fruit, and pictures of the toys. She had drawn pictures of the awards the doctor received and even one of the Presidential Medal of Freedom.

There were more drawings and paintings. There were many of him and Rufus. Pictures of Rufus and pictures of the doctor and Rufus playing. All the pictures of his life were in the brown paper bag.

"This is by far the best bag of them all," he whispered, and he closed his eyes.

## Epilog

As promised, here is a copy of the story that I wrote down right after the dream. I hope you decide that my book did the story I was told justice.

## The Brown Paper Bag

Some time ago there lived a young doctor. Across the street from this doctor lived a young child, much like you! The only difference I can remember is that the child was getting sicker and sicker every day.

All of the other doctors said. "It's the heart. There is nothing we can do!" No one had ever been able to help someone with this condition. They all said nothing can be done.

When our doctor noticed the child, he did an examination. The child asked,

# The Promise in a Brown Paper Bag

"Can you help me?" The doctor paused, but he did not say no. After thinking for a bit, the doctor simply answered, "We'll see".

Later at home the child said, "We'll see! we'll see! he said we'll see!" and the parent replied, "Yes, we'll see, is a very good answer."

We'll see, is a very good answer because it included hope, and hope is a very powerful thing.

The young doctor used that hope to start learning. He read all the books and papers and asked all the questions to the greatest doctors. "Perhaps", "maybe" and "possibly" were the answers that he was getting. All these words included hope.

The doctor realized the time had come to try to save the child's life. All he could still tell the child was "We'll see, but I have

b

hope" and all the child said was "I have hope too."

The doctor operated, the nurse wiped his brow. He worked and worked, cutting and sewing, the nurse wiped his brow again and again. After the surgery, everyone asked "did it work?" and "will the patient live?" "We'll see!" was the only thing the doctor could say.

In the days that followed, everyone saw. The parent saw, the nurse saw, even the doctor saw, the child was getting better.

The day came when the child was ready to be released from the hospital and could go home. This was also the day the family got the huge bill for the surgery. When the doctor came in to say goodbye, the child was sad because they didn't have the money to pay the huge bill. "All I can give you is this brown paper bag, and the promise I will put something in there for you". The child explained.

# The Promise in a Brown Paper Bag

"What will you put in there" the doctor asked? "We'll see" was the answer.

So, the doctor accepted a plain brown paper bag as his payment and set it outside his door wondering what will happen.

One day when he came home, the bag was filled with corn. The child's uncle had a farm and had plenty of sweet corn to share. The doctor ate delicious corn on the cob day after day and still had enough to give some to a poor family down the street.

From then on, the bag appeared over and over, filled with items the doctor could enjoy. Tomatoes, books and even a pair of slippers had been in the bag. The doctor had surprise after surprise. "This is the best payment of a bill I ever received," he thought.

Although the child was now almost grown, the bag continued to be filled

d

from time to time. One day the doctor discovered the old paper bag was full of toys. All of the toys from childhood were in the bag. There were happy meal toys and match book cars, teddy bears and action figures, filling the bag to the brim! "What will I do with all these toys", wondered the doctor. He decided to take them to the hospital and give them to all the children staying there.

All the nurses upon seeing the happy children, told the hospital president of what had happened. The hospital decided to give him an award. The doctor was so happy, but that turned out to be just the beginning. The story of the award spread far and wide. The important people investigated and found out that he had been helping children all along. He had helped many, many children and they decided to give him a promotion and a medal. The doctor had become famous, thanks to an old paper bag full of toys.

e

## The Promise in a Brown Paper Bag

The doctor thought that nothing could ever be in that old bag that could be better than the toys, but he was wrong. He was very wrong, because one day as he got home and walked to the porch, the paper bag was there, and it moved. He stopped in his tracks and watched carefully. Yes, the bag was moving! He heard a noise then rushed up to it and looked down inside. It was a puppy!

The puppy was perfect for the doctor who spent much of his time home alone. The puppy grew and grew and grew into being the doctor's best friend. Lonely at home no more, they played, learned tricks and both grew to love each other very much. "This was truly the greatest gift anyone could ever put in a bag. I couldn't possibly be wrong this time!" he said aloud to his dog. But there was still a thought in his head and it was "We'll see."

f

## The Promise in a Brown Paper Bag

Years past and now it was the doctor that was in the hospital. "There is nothing we can do" the doctors said. "We can't do anything to help you or say anything to make you happy". "There is just no hope" they all said. The only thing the doctor replied to them was, "We'll see."

Later that day he had a visitor, it was the child he had helped. The child of long ago had become an artist of great acclaim and was holding the brown paper bag. It was falling apart, but stuffed with pictures and paintings from over the years. It had been taped many times and had string holding it together at the top, but the contents were still overflowing. "This is the last time I will be able to fill up the bag" "I hope this covers the full cost of my debt to you." the great artist said quietly.

The doctor carefully opened and looked at the first picture in the bag. It was a drawing the child had made in the hospital and showed a handsome young doctor over the bed. There were more, lots more, each one more beautiful than the last. There were pictures of the doctor coming home from work, pictures of him working. Drawings and paintings of him eating corn! Lots of pictures of the corn. There were pictures of him getting awards and even one picture of the medal. More pictures and drawings, many of him and the dog, playing and sitting. All the pictures of his life were in the bag.

"This is by far the best bag of them all," he whispered, and he closed his eyes.

**The End**

# The Promise in a Brown Paper Bag

**TWISTED TRUTH PRESS**

www.ingramcontent.com/pod-product-compliance
Lightning Source LLC
Chambersburg PA
CBHW050829180626
46814CB00004B/1526